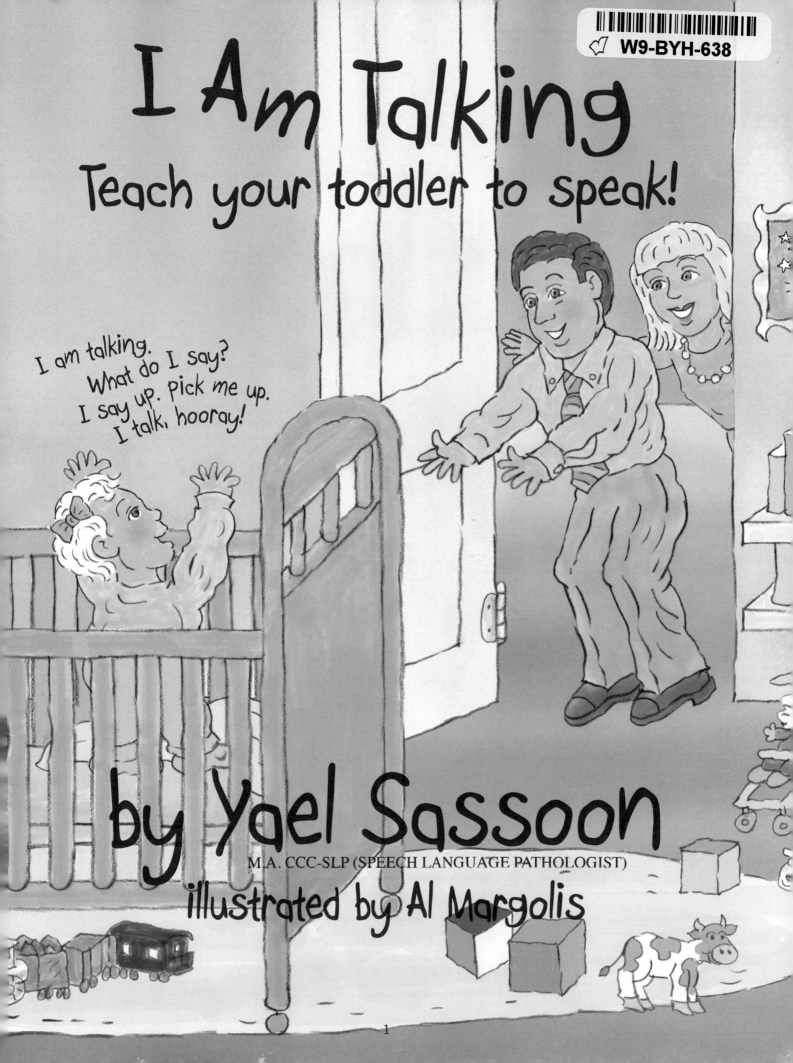

I Am Talking
Teach your toddler to speak!

I am talking.
What do I say?
I say up. pick me up.
I talk, hooray!

by Yael Sassoon
M.A. CCC-SLP (SPEECH LANGUAGE PATHOLOGIST)

illustrated by Al Margolis

1

Dear Moms, Dads, and Caregivers,

Timing of speech development varies greatly in babies and toddlers. In general, between six and eleven months of age, most babies begin to babble in imitation of real speech.

Your baby may begin saying a few words at twelve months. At around eighteen months, her vocabulary may reach between ten and twenty words, and she may even begin to combine simple words like "Daddy chair" (Daddy's in the chair). At twenty-four months old, her vocabulary jumps to about two hundred words, and by thirty-six months, her vocabulary will reach about nine hundred words.

This book's purpose is to encourage speech development from birth through the preschool years.

Enjoy your babies!

- Yael Sassoon

To my husband Eddie and
our amazing children:
Alan, Jojo, Robin and Emma

I Am Talking
Published, written and created by Yael Sassoon
Illustrated by Al Margolis
Name and characters are the product of the author's imagination, and any resemblance to actual persons
is entirely coincidental.

ISBN: 978-1483906263
ISBN: 1483906264

Published by Yael Sassoon

I am talking.
What do I say?
I say ma ma, ba ba, wa wa.
I talk, hooray!

I am talking.
What do I say?
I say more. More water.
I talk, hooray!

I am talking.
What do I say?
I say give me. Give me the ball.
I talk, hooray!

11

I am talking.
What do I say?
I say open. Open the box.
I talk, hooray!

I am talking. What do I say?
I say no more.
No more banana.
I talk, hooray!

I am talking.
What do I say?
I say good-bye. Good-bye, Mommy.
Good-bye, Daddy. I talk, hooray!

I am talking.
What do I say?
I say cow. Moo moo, cow.
I say sheep. Baa baa, sheep.
I talk, hooray!

I am talking.
What do I say?
I say eat. I eat soup.
I talk, hooray!

I am talking. What do I say?
I say _ _ _ _ _ _ I talk, hooray!

I am talking. What do I say?
I say sleep. I go to sleep.
Good night, Mommy. Good night, Daddy.
I talk, hooray!

Tips for encouraging children to speak:

1. "Ma ma, ba ba, wa wa"—Mimic the back-and-forth of conversation with your baby by copying his sounds. Keep the conversation going for as many turns as you can. Your baby will learn that when he makes a sound, you will respond.

2. "More"—Use of the word *more* expresses your child's early needs. Pour very little water in your child's cup on purpose so that she has to ask for more.

3. "Up"—As soon as your child makes a sound for the word *up,* immediately reward him by lifting him out of the crib, repeating the word *up* as you do. While it is ok (and developmentally appropriate) for your child to simplify words, you should use the correct pronunciation instead of repeating your child's simplification, like "wawa" for water.

4. "Give me"—Teach your child to use hand motions paired with words such as tapping her chest for "give me." This will help her understand the meaning of the words, and she will speak sooner. When your child points at a desired object, encourage her to include a sound or word instead of yelling or whining. Reward any attempt at sounds or words your child makes by granting the requested item quickly and with praise, hugs and kisses. Kids love "Hooray!" Repeat the target word, like "give me," as many times as you can. You can't overdo it.

5. "Open"—Follow your child's interests toward what he is reaching or wanting. He is more likely to talk about those things. Make opening a box a game, as if you need your child's help to open it. Encourage him to attempt the word *open* with even just a sound. Reward him by opening the box.

6. "No more"—Reward your child by removing the item she is finished with. Show your child that you respond to her talking and not to tantrums, yelling, or throwing things on the floor. By repeating back "no more grilled cheese," you are showing your child how to string words together.

7. "Good-bye"-Attach the word bye to people, objects and places you are leaving. For example, you can say, "Bye, Grandpa." This is an effective way for children to combine words and to transition from one activity to the next. *Bye-bye* is an appropriate version of good-bye.

8. "Go"—Sit on the floor and remain at eye level with your child during play. Tell different vehicles to "go," repeating the word *go* often. Always strive for a little bit more progress from your child by setting the bar a little higher. If your child already says *go*, encourage him to say "Go, car."

9. "Cow, moo; sheep, baa"—Children love animal sounds. Connect the word *cow*, and its sound, *moo*, with the animal by pointing to a picture, a toy or an actual cow. Remember children learn best by being able to see, hear, touch, and smell. Take advantage of new experiences by appealing to as many of your child's senses as possible when teaching her new words.

10. "Eat"—Attach your own tune to the phrase "I am talking." Then at meals and other times, you can use the tune in a playful manner to remind your child to use his words. Use meal times as an opportunity to name things that you are eating. Create phrases that are specific to you and your family. For example, "I am talking. What do I say? I say chicken. I talk, hooray!" Encourage progress by introducing a new word, better grammar or better pronunciation. As your child's speech matures, try, "I am eating. What do I eat? I eat chicken *and* broccoli. I eat, hooray!"

11. "In the bath"—Talk about the objects or people in the bath. Take advantage of location by asking your child simple "where" questions. For example "Where is the duck?" so she can answer "In the bath." These *where* questions can be used in other contexts, of course. For example, you can ask "Where are your shoes?" so she can answer "In the closet."

12. "Book, blocks, ball"—Name everything you see, in your home, as you walk down the street, at the supermarket and everywhere else you spend time with your child. For example, "I say flower. I talk, hooray!" Picking up the flower or touching it may be helpful when saying the word. Use dressing time as a time to label body parts.

13. "Sleep"—Pair the phrase "Good night" with important people in your child's life as well as objects in the room. Point to the objects as you bid them good night so that your child can learn their meaning. A variation would be to name people and things that are sleeping. For example, "The doll is sleeping."

About the author

Yael Sassoon M.A. CCC-SLP (SPEECH LANGUAGE PATHOLOGIST)

Yael and her husband, Eddie, live with their four children in Brooklyn, New York. She is a Speech Language Pathologist with a passion for speech development in young children. Yael hopes you enjoy being a part of your children's speech and language development as much as she did with her children. It is her hope that you can constantly invent new ways of incorporating I Am Talking into your daily lives.

About the illustrator

Al Margolis is a Cleveland Art School graduate; his career includes several years as an advertising agency art director, and is now owner of Margolis Creative, specializing in humorous illustration. Al's humorous illustrations have been used for both advertising and children's books. Helping children enjoy, learn, and understand their experiences is an important part of his work. Many more examples of his art can be seen at www.almargolis.com

Made in the USA
Charleston, SC
31 May 2013